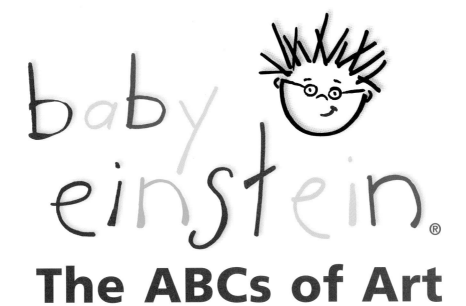

The ABCs of Art

By Julie Aigner-Clark

Illustrations by Nadeem Zaidi

For Sierra and Aspen . . .
Art is beautiful. It inspires.
It makes us think, feel, and react.
You are art.

Mommy

The publisher wishes to thank the following for their permission to reprint the artwork in this book:

Front cover:
Young Boy with Dog, by Pablo Picasso (1881–1973); © 2002 Estate of Pablo Picasso/Artists Rights Society (ARS), New York; transparency
    © Scala/Art Resource, New York

Back cover:
Reading, by Auguste Renoir (1841–1919); transparency © Réunion des Musées Nationaux/Art Resource, New York

Interior pages:
Detail of *Angel Annunciating,* by Lorenzo Lotto; transparency © Erich Lessing/Art Resource, New York
Ballon Rouge, by Paul Klee; © 2002 Artists Rights Society (ARS), New York/VG Bild-Kunst, Bonn; transparency © Girandon/Art Resource, New York
Cows, by Vincent van Gogh; transparency © Girandon/Art Resource, New York
Young Boy with Dog, by Pablo Picasso; © 2002 Estate of Pablo Picasso/Artists Rights Society (ARS), New York; transparency © Scala/Art Resource, New York
African Elephants, by Charles-Emile Vacher de Tournemine; transparency © Girandon/Art Resource, New York
Flag on an Orange Field, by Jasper Johns; © Jasper Johns/licensed by VAGA, New York; transparency © Girandon/Art Resource, New York
Reading, by Pierre-Auguste Renoir; transparency © Réunion des Musées Nationaux/Art Resource, New York
Little Blue Horse, by Marc Franz; transparency © Girandon/Art Resource, New York
Untitled (ice cream), by Andy Warhol; © 2002 The Andy Warhol Foundation for the Visual Arts/Artists Rights Society (ARS), New York; transparency
    © The Andy Warhol Foundation, Inc./Art Resource, New York
Monkidew, by Kenny Scharf; © 2002 Kenny Scharf/Artists Rights Society (ARS), New York; transparency © Art Resource, New York
Untitled (kite), by Andy Warhol; © 2002 The Andy Warhol Foundation for the Visual Arts/Artists Rights Society (ARS); transparency
    © The Andy Warhol Foundation, Inc./Art Resource, New York
Lion at Rest, by Rembrandt van Rijn; transparency © Girandon/Art Resource, New York
Sueno, by Alfredo Arreguin; transparency © Smithsonian American Art Museum, Washington, D.C./Art Resource, New York
Le Domaine d'Arnheim, by René Magritte; © 2002 C. Hersovici, Brussels/Artists Rights Society (ARS), New York; transparency
    © R. Magritte-ADAGP/Art Resource, New York
Octopus, by Alexander Calder; © 2002 Estate of Alexander Calder/Artists Rights Society (ARS); transparency © Art Resource, New York
Peacock, Anonymous; transparency © Victoria and Albert Museum, London/Art Resource, New York
The Ermine Portrait, by Nicholas Hillard; transparency © Victoria and Albert Museum, London/Art Resource, New York
Dream of a Storm at Dawn, by Charles E. Burchfield; transparency © Art Resource, New York
Winter, by Lucas van Valckenborch; transparency © Erich Lessing/Art Resource, New York
Buchenwald, by Gustav Klimt; transparency © Erich Lessing/Art Resource, New York
Children at the Ice Cream Stand, by William H. Johnson; transparency © Smithsonian American Art Museum, Washington, D.C./Art Resource, New York
Rustic Violinist with Little Girl, by Eastman Johnson; transparency © Art Resource, New York
Pileated Woodpecker, by John J. Audubon; transparency © Victoria and Albert Museum, London/Art Resource, New York
Fay Ray X Ray, by William Wegman; © 1994 William Wegman; reprinted by permission
Study for Homage to the Square: Departing at Yellow, by Josef Albers; © 2002 The Josef and Anni Albers Foundation/Artists Rights Society (ARS), New York;
    transparency © Tate Gallery, London/Art Resource, New York
Grevy's Zebra, by Andy Warhol; © Andy Warhol Foundation for the Visual Arts/Artists Rights Society (ARS), New York; courtesy Ronald Feldman FineArts, Inc./
    Art Resource, New York; transparency © The Andy Warhol Foundation, Inc./Art Resource, New York

For information address Hyperion Books for Children, 114 Fifth Avenue, New York, New York 10011-5690.
Printed in Singapore
ISBN 0-7868-0882-9
Library of Congress Catalog Card Number: 2002104207

Visit www.hyperionchildrensbooks.com and www.babyeinstein.com

Dear Parents,

As a child, I loved to draw. When asked what I wanted to be when I grew up, I always said, "a writer and an artist." Happily, I achieved one of these dreams. The other eluded me.

What I came to understand beyond childhood was that there was a difference between the drawing that we all try at one time or another—and art. I recognized this for the first time as a college student walking into the van Gogh Museum in Amsterdam. What I had thought would be a quick trip through the gallery became an entire day's outing that lasted into the next day, too.

I hadn't been raised in an environment that exposed me to art museums, nor did my most wonderful parents have any background in art, so what I discovered in this and the many museums I came to visit later was a world that had been invisible to me before—a world of thoughts and colors and history, a world I loved immediately upon entering.

Art is important. It records history without the barriers of language. It provides insights into the ways and customs of the people and places it depicts. It opens doors to the imagination and invites deeply personal interpretations by different viewers. Mostly, it's beautiful.

Children recognize this beauty instantly. They are drawn to color and subject, and they want to know the stories behind the images they see. The collection of paintings, lithographs, and sketches found in *The ABCs of Art* are drawn from an array of artists from a variety of periods. It is my great hope that I have given parents, grandparents, and caregivers who look through this book with children the opportunity to explore each work of art, to ask questions, and to engage their youngster in interesting conversations. Expand on the questions presented and encourage your child to find favorite pieces. Talk about color and light, and suggest that your child imagine stories to describe particular scenes or people within the paintings.

This is what art is about—sharing and exchanging ideas and experiencing the joy of beauty. It's what being a parent is all about, too. But you already knew that.

Jackie Aigner-Clark

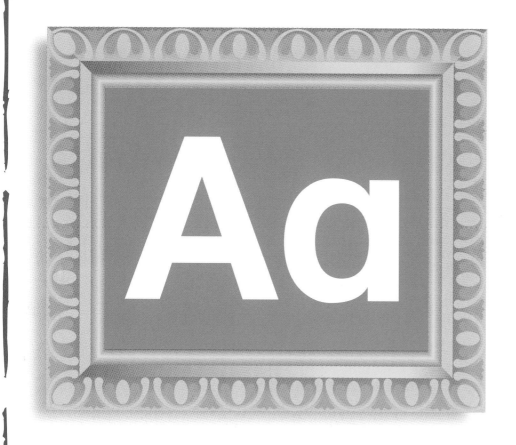

angel

A is for angel.

Look carefully.

What is the angel holding?

What makes this angel different from you?

Lorenzo Lotto (1480–1556), *Angel Annunciating*

balloon

B is for balloon.

Point to the balloon in the painting. What color is it?

The balloon is a circle shape. What other
shapes do you see?

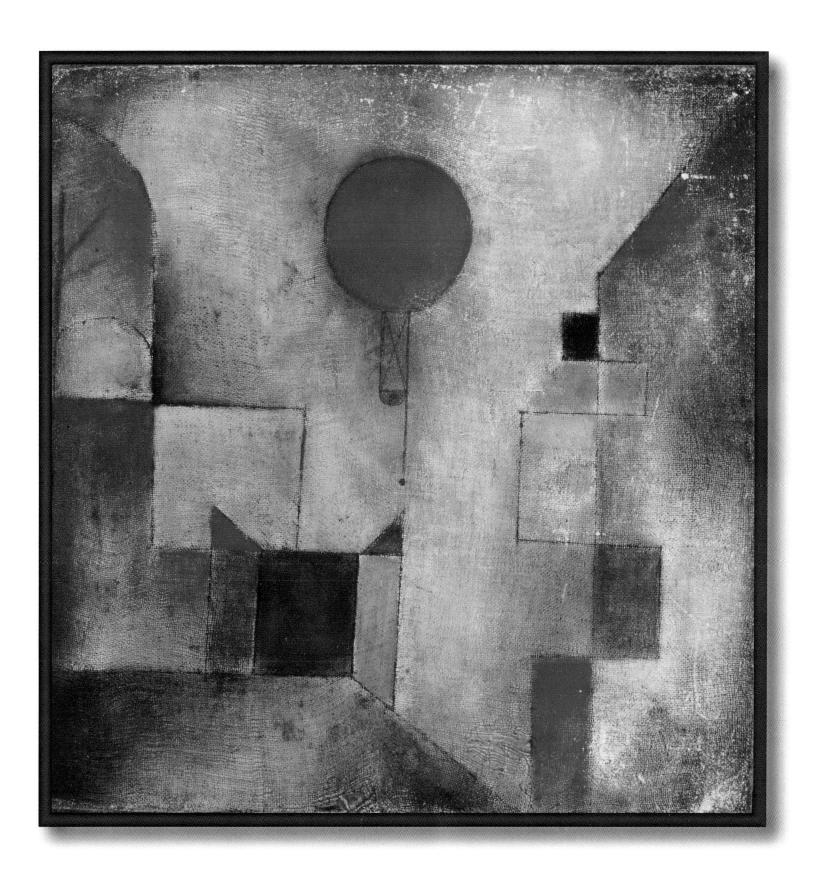

Paul Klee (1879–1940), *Ballon Rouge*

COWS

C is for cows.

Do you think it is spring, summer, fall, or winter in this painting?

What does the artist use more: curvy lines or straight lines?

Vincent van Gogh (1853–1890), *Cows*

dog

D is for dog.

What color does the artist use most in this painting?

What do you imagine the person and the dog are looking at?

Pablo Picasso (1881–1973), *Young Boy with Dog*

elephants

E is for elephants.

What time of day do you think it is in this painting?

If you were in this scene, what sounds might you hear?

Charles-Emile Vacher de Tournemine (1812–1872), *African Elephants*

flag

F is for flag.

What colors are in the American flag?

What shapes do you see in this painting?

Jasper Johns (b. 1930), *Flag on an Orange Field*

girls

G is for girls.

How do you think these girls know each other?
Do you think they're sisters? Friends?

What do you think would be nice names for these girls?

Pierre-Auguste Renoir (1841–1919), *Reading (La Lecture)*

horse

H is for horse.

Name five colors that you see in this painting.

Can you find mountains in the scene?

Franz Marc (1880–1916), *Little Blue Horse*

ice cream

I is for ice cream.

What shape is the cone? What shape is the ice cream?

Which two shades of color in the artwork are the most alike?

Andy Warhol (1928–1987), Untitled

jungle

J is for jungle.

Look carefully. Can you find two snakes?

If you could enter this painting, what would the scene smell like? Sound like? Feel like?

Kenny Scharf (b. 1958), *Monkidew*

kite

K is for kite.

What is it that keeps the kite from flying away?

Point to two things that are blue.

Andy Warhol (1928–1987), Untitled

lion

L is for lion.

What two colors are in this drawing?

How do you think this lion is feeling? Sleepy? Angry? Hungry?

Rembrandt van Rijn (1606–1669), *Lion at Rest*

monkeys

M is for monkeys.

How many monkeys do you see in this painting?

Where do you think these monkeys live?

Alfredo Arreguin (b. 1935), *Sueno (Dream)*

nest

N is for nest.

How many eggs are in this nest?

Look carefully. Can you find the outline of a bird with spread-open wings?

René Magritte (1898–1967), *Le Domaine d'Amheim (The Amheim Estate)*

octopus

O is for octopus.

What four colors do you see in this print?

Which of the objects do you think looks most like an octopus?

E.A.

Alexander Calder (1898–1976), *Octopus*

peacock

P is for peacock.

What do you think this peacock's feathers feel like?

What colors and shapes do you see in this bird?

Anonymous, c. 1830

queen

Q is for queen.

How can you tell that the woman in this painting is a queen?

Judging from her expression, how do you think the queen is feeling?

Nicholas Hillard (1547–1619), *The Ermine Portrait*

rainbow

R is for rainbow.

What colors do you see in the rainbow?

Can you see signs that some trees have been cut down?

Charles E. Burchfield (1893–1967), *Dream of a Storm at Dawn*

snow

S is for snow.

If you could enter this painting, what might you hear? How might you feel?

What clues tell you that this is a scene from a long time ago?

Lucas van Valckenborch (1530–1597), *Winter Landscape (February)*

trees

T is for trees.

What time of year do you think it is in this painting?

What animals do you think live in this forest?

Gustav Klimt (1862–1918), *Buchenwald (Beech Trees)*

umbrella

U is for umbrella.

Why is the man standing under an umbrella?

Where do you think this scene takes place?

William H. Johnson (1901–1970), *Children at the Ice Cream Stand*

violin

V is for violin.

What clues tell you this scene takes place outdoors?

What song do you imagine the man is playing for the little girl?

Eastman Johnson (1824–1906), *Rustic Violinist with Little Girl*

woodpeckers

W is for woodpeckers.

How many woodpeckers can you count on the tree?

Look carefully. Do you see a little worm?

John J. Audubon (1785–1851), *Pileated Woodpecker*

X ray

X is for X ray.

If you could name this dog, what would you call her?

Can you point to the X ray of the dog's spine?

William Wegman (b. 1943), *Fay Ray X Ray*

yellow

Y is for yellow.

How many different colored squares are in this painting?

Can you think of three things that are yellow?

Josef Albers (1888–1976), *Study for Homage to the Square: Departing in Yellow*

zebra

Z is for zebra.

What colors do you see that are not found on real zebras?

Are the zebra's stripes in perfectly straight lines?

Andy Warhol (1928–1987), *Grevy's Zebra.* Endangered species series

The Alphabet

Here's the whole alphabet for you to read and say.

A a   **B b**   **C c**

D d   **E e**   **F f**

G g   **H h**   **I i**   **J j**

K k   **L l**   **M m**   **N n**

O o   **P p**   **Q q**   **R r**

S s   **T t**   **U u**   **V v**

W w   **X x**

- What letters are shown in red?
- Which ones are blue?
- What capital and lower-case letters look the same?
- Which ones look different?

Y y   **Z z**

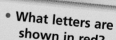

Ideas for Parents

Art appreciation and art creation enhance your child's life. Neither requires that you invest in great artwork nor that you stock your child's room with loads of top-grade supplies. Here are some ideas to make art a part of your child's everyday life in ways that mostly require only your time and encouragement:

- **Create an at-home art gallery.** Using a combination of your child's artwork, cutout pictures from magazines, and gift-shop museum postcard reproductions of great works of art, line a wall or two to create a personal museum. Encourage your child to lead you and other family members and friends on a guided tour of the works he or she has chosen to exhibit.

- **Make your own alphabet book.** Preschoolers will enjoy putting together their own *ABCs of Art* book, using any combination of their own artwork and reproductions gathered from magazines, books, or the museum store. Add commentary to the pages by transcribing your child's description of each piece.

- **Visit an art museum.** Find out when a local museum is most accommodating to young children. Some museums even set aside special times for family viewings. To help engage your child in the study of art, visit the gift shop and purchase a few postcards or other inexpensive reproductions of works on display and help your child hunt down each of the paintings or sculptures.

- **Explore a variety of media.** Help your child experience creativity in a number of different ways. Provide child-safe clay for sculpting. Create structures from cardboard, sticks, yarn, and other textiles.

- **Focus on the process, not just the result.** There's joy to be found in the act of creation itself. Engage in art activities that are not intended to be saved but savored during the creative process alone. For instance, on a warm day, invite your child to paint with plain water on the sidewalk. At the beach, join your child in sand sculpting or sand drawing.

- **Make specific collections.** Just for fun, create a series of drawings with your child, using only one colored crayon. Or create a series of self-portraits or landscapes. Encourage your child to consider in what ways works with similar styles or themes are alike, and in what ways are they different.

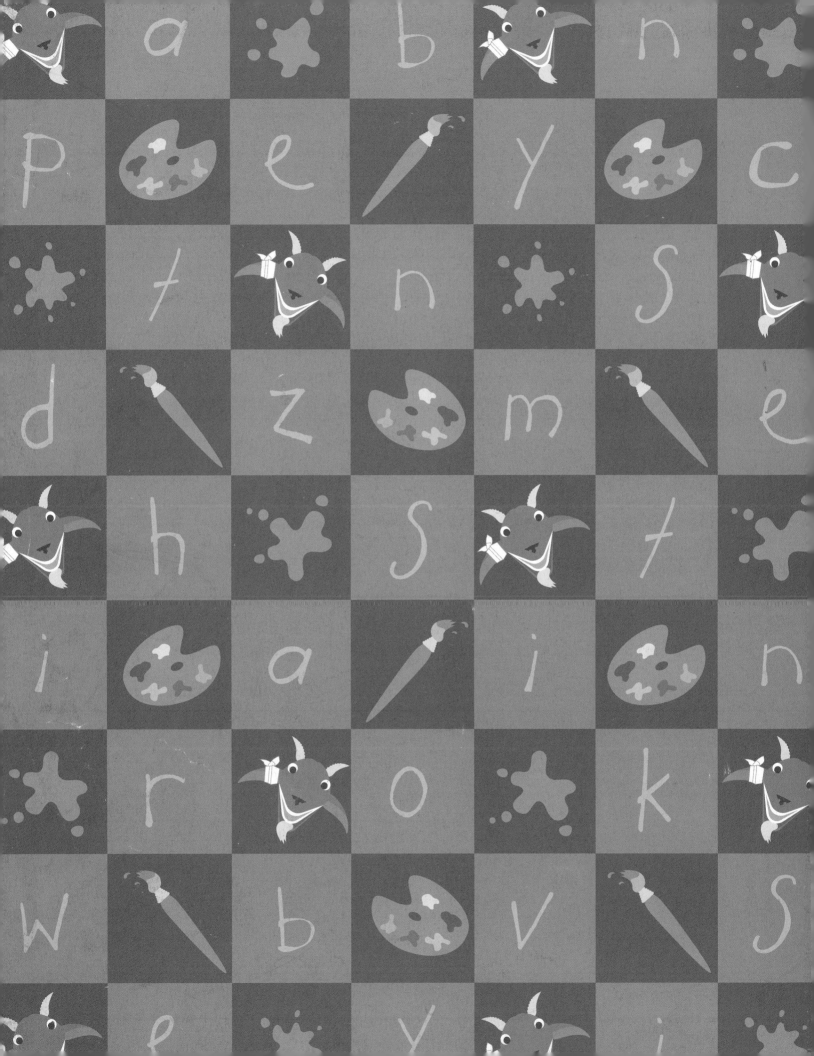